P9-CKS-143

WITHDRAWN

I Know Someone with

ADHD

Elizabeth Raum

THIS BOOK IS A GIFT
OF FRIENDS
OF THE ORINDA LIBRARY

Heinemann Library

Chicago, Illinois

www.heinemannraintree.com
Visit our website to find out more information about Heinemann-Raintree books.

To order:

☎ Phone 888-454-2279

💻 Visit www.heinemannraintree.com to browse our catalog and order online.

© 2011 Heinemann Library
an imprint of Capstone Global Library, LLC
Chicago, Illinois

All rights reserved. No part of this publication may be reproduced or transmitted in any form or by any means, electronic or mechanical, including photocopying, recording, taping, or any information storage and retrieval system, without permission in writing from the publisher.

Edited by Rebecca Rissman, Daniel Nunn, and Siân Smith
Designed by Joanna Hinton Malivoire
Picture research by Mica Brancic
Originated by Capstone Global Library
Printed in the United States of America by Worzalla Publishing

14 13 12 11 10
10 9 8 7 6 5 4 3 2 1

Library of Congress Cataloging-in-Publication Data
Raum, Elizabeth.
  I know someone with ADHD / Elizabeth Raum.
    p. cm. — (Understanding health issues)
  Includes bibliographical references and index.
  ISBN 978-1-4329-4553-4 (hc)
  ISBN 978-1-4329-4569-5 (pb)
  1. Attention-deficit hyperactivity disorder—Juvenile literature. I. Title.
  RJ506.H9R38 2011
  618.92'8589—dc22   2010026406

Acknowledgments
We would like to thank the following for permission to reproduce photographs: Corbis pp. 4 (Fancy/© Deborah Jaffe), 14 (© Klaus Tiedge), 27 (© STAFF/ Reuters); Getty Images pp. 6 (Blend Images/JGI/Jamie Grill), 9 (BLOOM image), 11 (Iconica/Peter Cade), 13 (The Image Bank/LWA), 17 (Digital Vision/Supernova), 18 (Dorling Kindersley/Steve Gorton), 19 (Riser/LWA), 20 (Photodisc/Sandy Jones), 21 (Photographer's Choice/Victoria Blackie), 23 (OJO Images/Anthony Lee), 24 (Photographer's Choice/Jeff Cadge), 25 (Stone/Michael Goldman), 26 (Bloomberg/Natalie Behring), 28 (The Image Bank/John Kelly); Photolibrary pp. 12 (Cultura/Monty Rakusen), 15 (Stockbroker/ Monkey Business Images Ltd), 22 (Cusp/LWA-Dann Tardif); Shutterstock pp. 5 (© Supri Suharjoto), 10 (© Suzanne Tucker).

Cover photograph of a boy painting reproduced with permission of Corbis (© Edith Held).

We would like to thank Matthew Siegel, Ashley Wolinski, and Professor Paul Cooper for their invaluable help in the preparation of this book.

Every effort has been made to contact copyright holders of any material reproduced in this book. Any omissions will be rectified in subsequent printings if notice is given to the publisher.

All the Internet addresses (URLs) given in this book were valid at the time of going to press. However, due to the dynamic nature of the Internet, some addresses may have changed, or sites may have changed or ceased to exist since publication. While the author and publisher regret any inconvenience this may cause readers, no responsibility for any such changes can be accepted by either the author or the publisher.

Contents

Some words are printed in bold, **like this**. You can find out what they mean in the glossary.

Do You Know Anyone with ADHD?

Do you have a friend who has trouble paying attention? Does your friend shout answers before the teacher finishes asking questions? Does your friend find it hard to sit still?

You cannot tell whether people have ADHD by looking at them.

Some children with ADHD feel the need to keep moving.

If so, your friend may have ADHD. Children with ADHD may have trouble **concentrating**, sitting still, or waiting patiently.

What Is ADHD?

Children with ADHD can find it difficult to **concentrate**.

"ADHD" is a word used by doctors, teachers, and parents. "ADHD" stands for "Attention-Deficit/Hyperactivity Disorder." This describes the different types of **behavior** that people with ADHD might show.

Some people with ADHD can find it hard to pay attention. They might find it difficult to think about one thing for a long time. They may jump from idea to idea or from one job to another.

Children with ADHD may:

- be forgetful
- be easily **distracted**
- have trouble completing tasks
- find it difficult to listen.

Children with ADHD can also be **impulsive**. Being impulsive means doing things suddenly without thinking about what might happen.

Children with ADHD may:
- interrupt others
- say things without thinking
- find it difficult to wait for their turn
- blurt out answers before the teacher has finished asking the question.

It can be hard for some children with ADHD to wait until the teacher calls on them.

Children with ADHD are not trying to cause trouble when they act without thinking ahead. It is more difficult for them to control impulsive **behavior** than it is for people without ADHD.

People with ADHD may also be **hyperactive**. Hyperactive people have a lot of energy. They find it difficult to sit still or be quiet for long periods of time.

Children with ADHD may sometimes:
- talk nonstop
- **fidget** or move all the time.

Resting quietly is difficult for hyperactive children.

Many children with ADHD enjoy being active.

Everyone acts in these ways sometimes. When people have ADHD, though, they show some or all of these **behaviors** a lot of the time.

Causes of ADHD

Scientists are studying the causes of ADHD.

Doctors do not know for certain what causes ADHD. But they do know that ADHD is not something you can catch like a cold. People with ADHD are as healthy as anyone else.

ADHD sometimes seems to run in families, kind of like having brown eyes or blonde hair. This means that certain people can be more likely to get ADHD. Scientists are investigating whether **chemicals** in the world around us can cause ADHD, too.

Some children with ADHD have a relative, often a parent, who also has ADHD.

Experts Decide

There is no one test for ADHD. Sometimes a child realizes that something is wrong and tells a parent or teacher. Sometimes the parent or teacher might notice the signs of ADHD.

One of the best things you can do when you are worried about something is to talk about it with someone you trust.

Parents and teachers work together with a doctor to decide if ADHD is the cause. If so, they figure out a plan. The plan may include working with a special teacher, getting extra help, or taking medicine.

Teachers or **psychologists** often help to decide if a child has ADHD.

ADHD Strengths

People with ADHD can be good at many things. They might be full of energy and enjoy having fun. Some other good qualities are listed below.

People with ADHD may be:
- good problem-solvers
- willing to try new things
- able to see things in new and interesting ways.

There is no **cure** for ADHD. Many teenagers and adults have it, too. As children grow older, they can learn to use their strengths and to manage any difficulties they might have.

Many children with ADHD go on to college.

Living with ADHD

It is important to be able to concentrate in school.

Children with ADHD may find school difficult. In school, teachers often need students to pay attention, sit still, and listen carefully. These kinds of **behaviors** are hard for children with ADHD.

Some children with ADHD find they can work better if they have some extra help in school. They may work with special teachers or assistants who help them to **concentrate** and complete their work.

Special teachers can provide extra help for children with ADHD.

Some people with ADHD find that keeping a list is a good way to remember things. Of course, no two people are alike. Everyone needs to find out what works best for him or her.

Calendars and diaries help us remember important dates.

Medicine helps some children with ADHD to do better in school.

Sometimes doctors give children with ADHD medicine to help them **concentrate**. Medicine may also help them control being **impulsive** or **hyperactive**. However, medicine is not right for everyone.

Being a Good Friend

Everyone needs a friend. A good friend values the things we do well. A good friend understands when we have problems and tries to help.

Good friends care about one another.

Friends make life better.

It is important to understand why people with ADHD might behave in certain ways, and to help other people to understand, too. The differences between us help to make life interesting.

Ways to Help

There are many ways you can help a friend with ADHD. Try not to **distract** your friend during class. Most of us find it easier to **concentrate** when it is quiet. This can be even more important for someone with ADHD.

Whispering makes it hard to concentrate on what the teacher is saying.

A good group works together to complete a project.

If you are working on a group project, find ways to help everyone do well. Break the project down into smaller jobs. Make sure everyone in the group understands what to do and when to do it.

Famous People

Children with ADHD often become successful adults. They find new ways to solve problems. They are not afraid to try new things.

Swimming champion Michael Phelps has ADHD.

Michael Phelps won eight gold medals at the 2008 Olympics.

U.S. swimmer Michael Phelps learned that he had ADHD when he was nine. He took medicine to help him succeed at school. Michael Phelps has become a world-champion swimmer.

ADHD: True or False?

Children with ADHD can be as bright as anyone else.

TRUE! Children with ADHD can be smart, creative, and good problem solvers—just like anyone else.

You can catch ADHD from someone who has it.

FALSE! It is not possible to catch ADHD.

For every 20 children around the world, 1 is likely to have ADHD.

TRUE! There is a good chance that someone in your class might have ADHD.

Glossary

behavior way of acting

chemicals materials that make up the world around us. Some chemicals, such as lead, cause problems if they are taken into the body.

concentrate give all your attention to something

cure medical treatment that makes someone better

distract disturb or draw attention away from something else

fidget move around restlessly

hyperactive restless, always moving, and unable to sit still for long periods

impulsive likely to act quickly without thought

psychologist person trained to treat people with ADHD and other learning or behavior difficulties

Find Out More

Books to Read

Robbins, Lynette. *How to Deal with ADHD (Kids' Health)*. New York: PowerKids, 2010.

Tourville, Amanda Doering. *My Friend Has ADHD*. Mankato, Minn.: Picture Window, 2010.

Websites

http://kidshealth.org/kid/
Visit Kids' Health and enter "ADHD" in the "Search here" box to learn more.

www.fffbi.com/info/academy.html
This site has games designed for children with ADHD.

Index

31901050421736